WAT
DOWN

Rabbits
in Danger

Other
Watership Down
fiction adventures

Escape to the Hills
Rabbits in Danger
We Need More Rabbits!
Challenge to Efrafa

Rabbits in Danger

Judy Allen

RED FOX

A Red Fox Book

Published by Random House Children's Books
20 Vauxhall Bridge Road, London SW1V 2SA

A division of The Random House Group Ltd
London Melbourne Sydney Auckland
Johannesburg and agencies throughout the world

www.watershipdown.net

Illustrations by County Studio, Leicester

1 3 5 7 9 10 8 6 4 2

Printed and bound in Denmark by Nørhaven A/S

THE RANDOM HOUSE GROUP Limited Reg. No. 954009

www.randomhouse.co.uk

ISBN 0 09 940365 X

This story represents scenes from
the television series, Watership Down,
which is inspired by Richard Adams'
novel of the same name.

Contents

The Characters of Watership Down

Hazel

The leader of the group, Hazel persuaded his friends to leave their old warren at Sandleford and start a new life elsewhere.

Fiver

One of the youngest rabbits, Hazel's brother Fiver has visions of the future – a gift that sometimes causes him many problems.

Bigwig

A former member of the Sandleford Owsla, Bigwig naturally uses force to settle any disputes and has no time for time-wasters.

Pipkin

The youngest and most vulnerable rabbit, Pipkin is innocent, sweet and adventurous, and a well-loved friend to all the group.

Blackberry

An intelligent doe, Blackberry is a great problem solver and at times of crisis, she is the calm voice of reason.

Hawkbit

Hawkbit is always ready to look on the glum side, but when the going gets tough, his loyalty to the group shines through.

Dandelion

Talker, joker and storyteller, Dandelion is always ready to celebrate the heroic deeds of the warren and El-Arah.

Kehaar

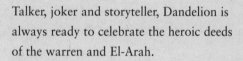

A newcomer to the group, Kehaar thinks he's much cleverer than the rabbits, but infact he can't manage without them.

Hannah

A fearless fieldmouse, Hannah often tends to forget her size and has no problem trading insults with bigger animals.

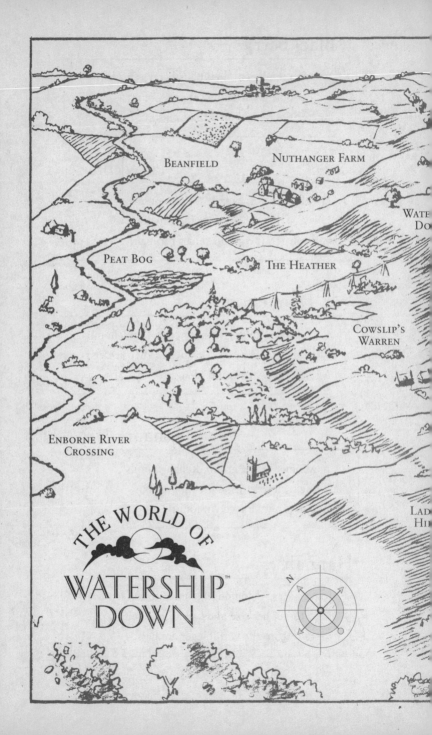

BEANFIELD

NUTHANGER FARM

WATE
DO

PEAT BOG

THE HEATHER

COWSLIP'S
WARREN

ENBORNE RIVER
CROSSING

THE WORLD OF

WATERSHIP
DOWN

LAD
HI

N

CHAPTER ONE

The Search for Pimpernel

High on Watership Down, Hazel and Bigwig were watching the sunrise. Hazel's younger brother Fiver was sitting beside Holly, who was still asleep, exhausted by his escape from Sandleford warren. Pipkin, Hawkbit and Dandelion were nibbling the rich grass.

Blackberry was burrowing under the roots of the old beech tree, soil flying out behind her as she worked.

'Come on,' said Hazel. 'It's time we all joined in.'

'Digging is doe's work!' said Bigwig.

Blackberry's muffled voice came out of the hole. 'I can't build the warren on my own,' she said.

'You won't have to,' said Hazel. He stared at the other rabbits until Hawkbit, Dandelion and Pipkin stopped eating and started digging.

Kehaar the gull waddled over. 'You find worms?' he said hopefully.

'We'll try,' sighed Pipkin.

'I can hardly believe our warren at Sandleford was destroyed' said Hazel. 'Holly was lucky to escape.'

'We all were,' said Bigwig. 'I'm glad you and Fiver made us leave.'

'Fiver's vision was right,' said Hazel.

Bigwig nodded. 'But that doesn't mean he's right about everything,' he said.

'Never said I was,' said Fiver, hopping up to them.

'How's Holly this morning?' asked Bigwig.

'Still weak,' said Fiver. 'But he wants to go back to the warren where he left Pimpernel and bring him here.'

'He's a true Owsla captain,'
said Bigwig, approvingly. 'More
concerned for his troops than
himself.'

'Holly should rest,' said Hazel.

'Well why don't we go and fetch
Pimpernel ourselves?' said Bigwig.
'It would be interesting to see
another warren.'

Hazel looked thoughtful. 'Perhaps we should,' he said. At once he was surrounded by Fiver, Hawkbit, Dandelion and Pipkin, all wanting to go too.

'Sorry,' said Hazel. 'Some of you must help Blackberry.'

He chose Fiver and Bigwig, and led the expedition down the hill. They had not gone far when Holly caught up with them, limping slightly.

'Holly,' said Hazel. 'I don't think you're strong enough.'

'Of course he is!' said Bigwig.

'Who's in charge here?' said Holly, puzzled.

'Hazel,' muttered Bigwig.

'All right, Holly,' said Hazel quickly, to save Bigwig's feelings. 'You can come.'

They moved slowly, stopping often to sniff the air for danger. By the time they'd crossed the fields of the farm below, and travelled through the woods beyond, it was evening, and storm clouds were gathering.

In front of them lay a huge warren, dug into a curved bank topped by trees. Outside sat two large sleek rabbits.

'The bigger one's Cowslip,' said
Holly. 'He's their leader. The other
one's Strawberry.'

'It's a huge place!' said Hazel.

'Looks as if there'd be room for us, if we wanted to move in,' said Bigwig.

Fiver shivered.

'What is it?' said Hazel.

'I'm not sure,' said Fiver.

The first drop of rain fell.

'We may be able to spend the night in a dry burrow,' said Hazel. 'Come on.'

As he hopped towards them, Cowslip and Strawberry stood up

and bowed. Then they circled the Watership Down rabbits in a slow dance.

'Welcome, welcome, greetings all,' said Cowslip. 'It's so nice of you to call.' He reached out a paw and patted Hazel and Bigwig.

They drew back in alarm, but Holly whispered, 'It's all right, it's something they all do when they meet.' Aloud he said, 'We've come for Pimpernel.' Cowslip didn't seem to hear. 'Come in out of the rain,' he said. 'Soft and sweet though it is...'

The rabbits followed him into the warren. Bigwig looked around at the smooth walls and high ceilings.

'Most impressive,' he said.

The first lightning flash of the storm lit the burrow-opening behind them, and Fiver shuddered. 'There's something wrong here,' he said.

'You're just tired,' said Hazel. 'Things will look better in the morning.'

Fiver looked round, his eyes wide and startled. 'Morning feels a long way away,' he said.

CHAPTER TWO

Cowslip's Warren

The Watership Down rabbits had never seen anything like Cowslip's warren. The central burrow was amazingly high and wide. There was an unusually large store of cabbages and carrots. Most surprising of all, one of the walls was decorated with stones and bits of coloured glass.

Hazel couldn't help staring.

'We don't have to worry about enemies or finding food,' explained Strawberry, 'so we have time to make pretty things.'

All the warren rabbits were large and sleek. They watched in silence as Strawberry and Cowslip showed the newcomers around.

'They look sad and sort of lost,' whispered Fiver.

'They look healthy and well-fed to me,' said Hazel.

'And the burrows are dry,' said Holly, 'even though it's raining outside.'

Bigwig turned to Cowslip. 'So where's Pimpernel?' he said.

'Good friends,' said Cowslip smoothly, ignoring the question. 'Please eat. Help yourselves. We have plenty.'

'Where do you get all this flayrah?' said Bigwig.

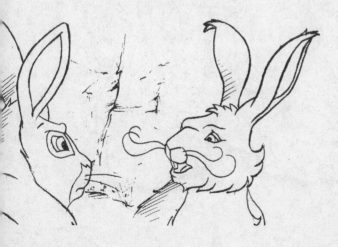

'Tomorrow,' said Cowslip.
'Tomorrow you'll see.' He moved to
the middle of the burrow. 'Good
friends, attend!' he called. 'We have
entertainment! The sweet rhymes
of Silverweed.'

'That Cowslip's got an odd way with words,' muttered Bigwig.

The warren rabbits formed a circle with Silverweed in the centre.

'He smells of dead leaves,' Fiver whispered to Hazel.

Silverweed raised his voice in an eerie chant. 'Frith, the Great Sun, lies in the evening sky. Take me with you, Lord Frith, to the heart of the light...'

'I don't like this,' Fiver shivered.

Silverweed stared straight at him, and his voice sang on, 'I am ready, Lord Frith, to give you my breath – my life –'

'No!' shouted Fiver. 'Let me out of here!' And he ran.

Hazel and Bigwig followed him
outside, into the rain.

'What is the matter?' said Bigwig.
'There's sadness and fear in that
place,' said Fiver, shuddering.

Neither Hazel nor Bigwig could persuade him to come back inside. Reluctantly, they returned without him.

'I'll try again later,' said Hazel, but the burrow was warm and they had eaten well. Soon he, Bigwig and Holly were sound asleep.

They were startled awake at dawn by a terrifying scent.

'There's a fox outside!' said Bigwig.

A single shot rang out.

'And a Man!' said Holly.

Cowslip appeared beside them. 'We're safe, friends,' he said smoothly. 'The Man killed the fox for us. He's gone now.'

Hazel looked wildly around. 'Fiver's still out there!' he said.

He and Bigwig found Fiver under a yew tree. The rain had stopped, but he was very cold.

'This is an evil place,' said Fiver. 'Let's go home.'

'We have to find Pimpernel first,' said Hazel.

'You won't,' said Fiver sadly. 'He's gone.'

'Nonsense!' said Bigwig. Then he spotted Cowslip,

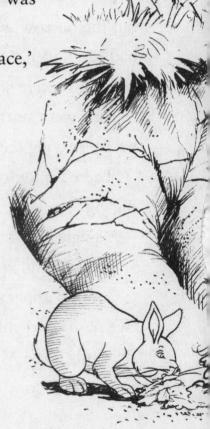

Strawberry and the other warren
rabbits. They were eating a pile of
lettuces and carrots nearby.

Bigwig and Hazel hopped
over to them. Fiver
followed slowly.

'Where does all
this come from?'
said Hazel.

'Man leaves it,' said Cowslip.
'You'll enjoy life here.'

'We only came for Pimpernel,' said
Hazel. 'We're not staying long.'

'Long, short,' said Cowslip,
drifting away, 'you never know...'

Holly bounded up. 'I can't find
Pimpernel anywhere,' he said. 'And
no one will tell me anything.'

'There's something horribly wrong
with this place,' said Fiver.

'Stop moaning, Fiver!' said Bigwig.
'Cowslip's invited me to stay and, by
Frith, I think I will!' He bounded off
through an opening in the hedge. A
second later a yell of pain and fear
made them all jump.

Hazel reached Bigwig first. He
was lying on his side, a wire noose
around his neck. 'Hazel!' he choked.
'I'm trapped! Help me!'

CHAPTER THREE

The Shining Wires

The more Bigwig struggled, the more the noose tightened around his neck.

Hazel saw that the wire was fixed to a peg in the ground. He sent Holly for help while he and Fiver worked to dig it out.

Holly ran to the warren rabbits.

'Cowslip! Strawberry!' he panted.
'Bigwig's caught in a shining wire!'

The warren rabbits stared at him.
No one moved.

'Didn't you hear me!' shouted
Holly. 'Bigwig's trapped!'

'There is no Bigwig,' said Cowslip, turning away. 'There never was.'

'You're mad,' said Holly. He raced back to Hazel and Fiver, just as they got the peg clear. 'The others won't come!' he gasped.

'It's all right,' said Hazel, lifting the wire loop over Bigwig's head. 'He's free!'

But Bigwig didn't get up. He lay still, his eyes closed.

'We're too late,' said Holly.

'Oh, Bigwig!' said Fiver.

'My friend has stopped running,' said Hazel, his eyes filled with grief.

'The shining wires are everywhere,' said Fiver. 'Cowslip knows about them. They all do.'

'The Man will come soon,' said a sorrowful voice. 'He'll take Bigwig away.' Strawberry was beside them, his head bowed in shame.

Holly glared at him. 'That's what happened to Pimpernel, isn't it?' he said. 'The wire got him.'

'When a rabbit is gone,' said Strawberry miserably, 'we never speak his name again. The Man feeds us and protects us from the fox. This is the price we pay.'

'Why in Frith's name didn't you warn us?' said Hazel.

'If the wire took you,' said Strawberry, his voice shaking, 'we'd live one day longer.'

'I'll kill the lot of them!' said Bigwig, staggering to his feet.

'Bigwig!' said Hazel.

'You're alive!' said Fiver.

'Yes,' said Bigwig, 'but I want a word with Cowslip. Come on!'

He marched back to the warren, Hazel and Fiver on one side of him, Holly on the other.

'Go away,' said Cowslip, as they approached. 'Unless you want to fight.'

'You've forgotten how!' said
Bigwig scornfully.

Cowslip leapt at him, clawing and
scratching. Despite Cowslip's size,
Bigwig swatted him aside as easily as
if he'd been a fly.

As Cowslip struggled to his feet, Hazel said, 'You must all leave or the snares will get you.'

Cowslip backed slowly into the warren. His voice came out of the darkness. 'They won't get me,' he said, and he laughed. 'Others, maybe – never me.'

Hazel shuddered. 'Run!' he said. 'We have to get away from here.'

They raced back through the woods and fields and didn't stop until they reached the foot of Watership Down.

'Fiver,' said Bigwig, as they rested. 'I'm sorry, I should have listened to you.'

'We should all have listened,' said
Holly.

The long grass rustled and parted.
Strawberry stood in front of them,
his eyes wide with fear. 'Take me
with you,' he begged.

'Why should we?' snarled Bigwig.
'You lied to us.'

'We're not allowed to tell the truth,' said Strawberry. 'I was afraid. Don't make me go back.'

'It's too late to help Pimpernel,' said Hazel. 'But we can save Strawberry.'

Fiver and Holly nodded.

'All right,' said Bigwig. 'Let's get moving.'

As they climbed the hill, Kehaar
flew to meet them, with Hannah the
fieldmouse riding on his back. 'We
beat you home, yes?' he squawked,
gliding ahead.

'Home,' said Strawberry, happily.

Dandelion, Pipkin and Hawkbit appeared on the crest above, muddy and cross.

'We hope you've had a nice time,' said Dandelion.

'Because we haven't,' said Pipkin.

'We're soaked and Blackberry won't give us a moment's rest,' said Hawkbit.

Hazel sighed. 'Home, sweet home!' he said.

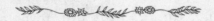

CHAPTER FOUR

Digging or Training

Deep under the beech tree,
Hazel, Blackberry and Fiver
were digging hard. Lower down the
hill, Bigwig, who had recovered from
his ordeal with the shining wire, was
shouting military commands at
Hawkbit, Dandelion and Pipkin.

Between the two, Strawberry was
dreaming in the soft grass.

He opened his eyes to see Hazel
beside him. 'Hazel,' he said, 'I'm so
happy I left Cowslip's warren. Here,
you're all free!'

'We may be free,' said Hazel,
'but we have to work to survive.
Shouldn't you be training with
Bigwig?'

Blackberry appeared beside him.
'Or digging with us?' she said.

'Everything sounds so tiring,' said
Strawberry.

'I'm calling a meeting,' said Hazel.
'We need more diggers.'

Kehaar and Hannah were
surprised to find all eight rabbits
sitting under a walnut tree.

'Is big gathering,' said Kehaar.

'Why didn't anyone tell us?' said
Hannah.

'Ssh!' said Fiver.

'I don't dig,' announced Bigwig.

'My job is defence.'

'Until we build the warren, what is there to defend?' said Blackberry.

'Our lives!' said Bigwig. 'Strawberry's told me about a vicious, bloodthirsty warren nearby, called Efrafa.'

'Strawberry?' said Hazel. 'Have you seen this warren?'

'No,' said Strawberry. 'But I've heard stories.'

A walnut fell from the tree above onto Hannah's head. She squealed, and Kehaar shouted, 'We under attack!'

Hazel ignored them. 'Bigwig,' he said, 'We have no proof these stories are true.'

'All right,' said Bigwig. 'I'll get proof. You dig and I'll go on solitary patrol.'

'We come, too!' shrieked Kehaar.

'No,' said Bigwig, marching off. 'Solitary means alone.'

Fiver shivered. 'Bigwig,' he said. 'Be careful.'

He had little time to worry. Blackberry immediately organised two work parties, Fiver and Pipkin

digging inside with her, Hazel and
Hawkbit digging outside, to make
a new entrance.

Somehow, Strawberry managed
not to dig with either group.

'He's useless!' said Hawkbit.

'He had life easy in Cowslip's
warren,' said Hazel. 'He'll learn our
ways soon.'

'Hmm!' said Hawkbit. 'Well, right now he's asleep in the clover!'

When Bigwig returned, his fur was dirty and ruffled and he was breathing hard.

'They nearly caught me!' he said.

'Who?' said Hazel, as the rabbits gathered around.

'I spotted an Efrafan patrol,' said Bigwig. 'They know about us! They plan to find our warren and wipe us out.'

'Are you sure?' said Hazel.

'Certain!' said Bigwig. 'I got close enough to overhear them. Then they saw me and I had to run for my life. Every rabbit must be trained to defend the warren!'

'But Blackberry's right,' said Hazel, 'we have to dig, too. We'll split up as before. Fiver and I with Blackberry. Hawkbit, Dandelion and Pipkin with you.'

'I suppose half an Owsla is better than nothing,' grumbled Bigwig.

'We volunteer for Oozley,' said Kehaar.

Hannah nodded. 'I've got a plan with walnuts,' she said.

'Certainly not,' said Bigwig.

'But Hannah has interesting ideas,' said Blackberry. 'And Kehaar could scout from the sky.'

'It's rabbits only,' said Bigwig.

'And speaking of rabbits, where's Strawberry?'

'Here,' yawned Strawberry.

'You don't enjoy digging,' said Hazel. 'You'd better join the Owsla.'

'Right, troops!' said Bigwig. 'Pay attention. You were useless in training. This time you'll have to learn in action.'

'You mean real action?' said Pipkin, alarmed.

'I do,' said Bigwig. 'We're going to find the Efrafans and get a closer look at them. Forward!'

CHAPTER FIVE

Bigwig's Patrol

Bigwig led the way, with Hawkbit, Dandelion and Pipkin following. It wasn't long before they had to go back for Strawberry. Bigwig found him asleep in the grass.

'I'm sorry,' said Strawberry, scrambling to his feet. 'It won't happen again!'

'No, it won't!' said Bigwig. 'Because you're discharged! Go back! Now!'

Strawberry walked away, his ears drooping. 'I didn't help dig, and I'm not wanted in the Owsla,' he said to himself. 'They'll banish me from the warren.' He paused. 'Unless I change! I will! I'll go back and dig and dig –' He began to run.

The rest of the patrol moved on with Bigwig.

Suddenly a line of mean-looking rabbits appeared on a hilltop ahead.

'Efrafans!' said Bigwig. 'The ones I saw before!'

'Shall we go back?' said Pipkin nervously.

'We can't!' said Bigwig. 'We'd lead them to Watership Down. Quick! Scatter!'

They ran at full speed, bobbing and weaving through the grass as the Efrafans swept down the hill towards them.

They raced through a field, under a hedge, then along the side of a road. They'd had a good start, but the

Efrafans were gaining on them.
Then Bigwig spotted a drainage
tunnel that crossed under the road.
'Come on!' he shouted, leading
the way in. But Pipkin,
running behind the
others, saw something
Bigwig had missed.
The other end of the
tunnel was blocked,
and the Efrafans
were already
bounding towards
the entrance.
'We're trapped!'
said Dandelion.

'Where's Pipkin?' said Hawkbit.

As he spoke, Pipkin raced past the entrance of the tunnel, right in front of the Efrafans.

'Get him!' yelled their leader, and the entire Efrafan patrol raced off in pursuit. Bigwig, Dandelion and

Hawkbit stumbled out of the dark tunnel.

'Pipkin's leading them away!' said Bigwig. 'Hawkbit, you and Dandelion run back to the warren!'

'What about Pipkin?' said Dandelion.

'I'll find him!' said Bigwig.

He caught up with the chase just as Pipkin fell, surrounded by hostile rabbits. As Bigwig prepared to charge, a fearsome screech rang out from above and Kehaar swooped out of the sky. On his back sat Hannah, pelting the Efrafans with walnuts.

The Efrafans dived for cover, and Bigwig grabbed Pipkin and dragged him to safety.

By the time the Efrafans had staggered to their feet, Bigwig and Pipkin were out of sight, running steadily for home.

Kehaar flew above, with Hannah clinging to his neck. 'Hey, Bigwig!' she called.

'You much proud of us?' shrieked Kehaar.

'Yes,' puffed Bigwig. 'Good work, you two.'

Back on Watership Down, the other rabbits watched anxiously as earth came showering out of a new burrow under the beech tree.

'Strawberry, stop!' shouted Hazel. 'It isn't safe.'

'You're digging at the wrong angle,' called Blackberry.

'Must dig,' came a muffled voice. 'Have to dig. Love to dig.'

At that moment, the whole

burrow caved in on top of him.

'Quick!' cried Hazel, and he, Blackberry and Fiver scraped frantically at the soil until Dandelion and Hawkbit could pull Strawberry clear.

'I'm sorry to be a nuisance,' said Strawberry, shaking earth out of his ears. 'I wanted to prove myself. I was afraid you'd send me away.'

'Never,' said Hazel. 'You're one of us.'

'Hazel!' called Bigwig, as he and Pipkin reached the foot of the tree. 'Those Efrafan rabbits are even more dangerous than I thought. We must do more work here. We need secret entrances – hiding places – traps.'

'And who's going to do all this?' asked Blackberry.

'I and my Owsla!' said Bigwig.

'I thought you said burrow-building was doe's work,' said Hazel.

'This is different,' said Bigwig. 'This is essential military defence.'

And, to everyone's amazement, he began to dig.

Glossary

Buck   A male rabbit

Doe   A female rabbit

Efrafa   The name of General Woundwort's warren

El-Arah   The shortened name of the rabbit hero, El-ahrairah. The many stories of El-Arah are an inspiration to all rabbits

Elil   Enemies of rabbits; like foxes, hawks and weasels

Flayrah   Good food; like carrots, cabbages and lettuces

Frith   The sun; a god to the rabbits

Frithmas   The rabbits' Christmas celebration; it is celebrated with a great feast

Inle   The moon; when it is time for a rabbit to die, the Black Rabbit of Inle comes to fetch him

Owsla   A group of strong brave rabbits who are trained to defend the warren

Silflay   Eating outside the warren; usually at dawn or dusk

Warren   The network of burrows where rabbits live

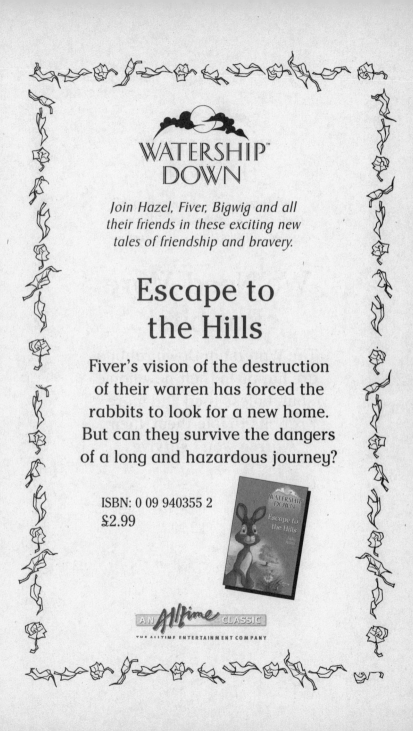

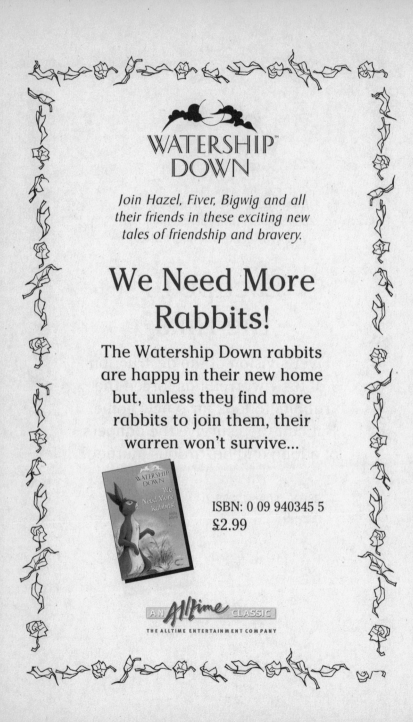

WATERSHIP™ DOWN

Join Hazel, Fiver, Bigwig and all their friends in these exciting new tales of friendship and bravery.

Challenge to Efrafa

The Watership Down rabbits decide to help the unhappy rabbits at Efrafa to escape. But to do this they need to outwit the evil General Woundwort...

ISBN: 0 09 940335 8
£2.99

WATERSHIP™ DOWN

*Join Hazel, Fiver, Bigwig and all
their friends in these exciting new
tales of friendship and bravery.*

COMING SOON

The Hidden World

When Hazel, Hawkbit and
Fiver fall down a hole in their
warren, they find themselves
buried in an underground
tunnel. But where does it lead
and can they find a way out?

AVAILABLE MARCH 2000

WATERSHIP DOWN

*Join Hazel, Fiver, Bigwig and all
their friends in these exciting new
tales of friendship and bravery.*

COMING SOON

Friend and Foe

The threat from Efrafa is
growing all the time. So
when Hazel finds the captain
of their Owsla wounded, he
tries to make friends with
him and bring him round to
their way of thinking.

AVAILABLE MARCH 2000